KATIE KAZOO, SWITCHEROO

Be Nice to Mice!

by Nancy Krulik • illustrated by John & Wendy

Grosset & Dunlap

For Sarah and Emily—NK
For our wonderful friends at the
Central Park Zoo—J&W

GROSSET & DUNLAP
Published by the Penguin Group
Penguin Group (USA) Inc., 375 Hudson Street,
New York, New York 10014, U.S.A.
Penguin Group (Canada), 90 Eglinton Avenue East, Suite 700,
Toronto, Ontario, Canada M4P 2Y3
(a division of Pearson Penguin Canada Inc.)
Penguin Books Ltd, 80 Strand, London WC2R 0RL, England
Penguin Ireland, 25 St Stephen's Green, Dublin 2, Ireland
(a division of Penguin Books Ltd)
Penguin Group (Australia), 250 Camberwell Road,
Camberwell, Victoria 3124, Australia
(a division of Pearson Australia Group Pty Ltd)
Penguin Books India Pvt Ltd, 11 Community Centre,
Panchsheel Park, New Delhi - 110 017, India
Penguin Group (NZ), Cnr Airborne and Rosedale Roads,
Albany, Auckland 1310, New Zealand
(a division of Pearson New Zealand Ltd)
Penguin Books (South Africa) (Pty) Ltd, 24 Sturdee Avenue,
Rosebank, Johannesburg 2196, South Africa

Penguin Books Ltd, Registered Offices:
80 Strand, London WC2R 0RL, England

Library of Congress Control Number: 2005024305

ISBN 978-0-448-44132-0   10 9 8 7 6 5

Chapter 1

"This is the prettiest lightning bug ever!" Katie Carew exclaimed. She looked down at the papier-mâché insect she and her friend Emma Weber had built and smiled proudly.

"I think so, too," Emma agreed. She sprinkled some glitter on one of the bug's wings.

"Wait until everybody sees our finishing touch," Katie added with a grin. She held up a small pocket flashlight and tucked it into a little hole in the back of the bug. "Now our lightning bug can really glow!" Katie made the light flicker on and off. It looked just like a real lightning bug.

"We're sure to win a prize at the science fair!" Emma declared.

But Katie wasn't as confident. As she looked around their classroom she could see that other kids in class 4A were buzzing with as much excitement about their projects as she and Emma were.

The fourth-graders had been studying insects in class. Now they had paired up to do a project for the school science fair on Friday. Each pair was building a bug and creating a fact poster.

"Mr. Guthrie sure went buggy decorating the classroom," Emma laughed, glancing up at all the paper dragonflies, bees, and mosquitoes their teacher had hung from the ceiling.

"I know," Katie agreed, looking down at her feet. Mr. Guthrie had taped paper ants and cockroaches to the floor. "Good thing I'm not scared of bugs."

In fact, no one in Katie's class was scared of bugs. They'd been studying them for so long that the kids were kind of used to them. Recently they had decorated their beanbag chairs with wings, antennae, and six cardboard tube legs. During science week they could sit in *beanbugs* at school.

"Wouldn't it be great if we could bring real insects to the science fair?" Kevin Camilleri asked his partner, George Brennan.

"That would be so cool!" George agreed.

Katie rolled her eyes. That probably *wouldn't* be too cool, especially since George and Kevin were studying cockroaches. Even though Katie wasn't afraid of insects, she didn't necessarily want an army of cockroaches roaming their classroom.

"Maybe we should put some leftover food around our cockroach to show what they eat," Kevin suggested. "We could get some stale bread or moldy chocolate cake or something."

"I don't think that's such a great idea, dude," Mr. Guthrie interrupted. "It might bring some *real* insects to our classroom."

"That's exactly what we were hoping for!" Kevin exclaimed.

"Let's just stick to pipe cleaners and clay," Mr. G. said with a laugh.

Katie looked over at Kevin and George's project. The boys had built their huge brown bug from clay. They'd used black pipe cleaners for its six legs and antennae.

"If this were a real cockroach, it would be a giant!" George said. "The king of the cockroaches."

"I wish this thing would come alive just like Frankenstein's monster," Kevin agreed. "Then George and I would definitely win the blue ribbon at the science fair!"

Katie gulped. Kevin had just made a wish. That was *so* not good!

5

Chapter 2

Katie was an expert on wishes. She knew that they sometimes came true . . . and not the way you expected them to. In fact, the way some wishes came true could be really awful!

Katie learned that lesson the hard way. It happened one horrible day back in third grade. Katie had lost the football game for her team. Then she'd splashed mud all over her favorite jeans. But the worst part of the day came when Katie let out a loud burp—right in front of the whole class. It had been so embarrassing!

That night, Katie made a wish that she could be anyone but herself. There must have been a shooting star overhead when she made the wish, because the very next day the magic wind came.

The magic wind was a really powerful tornado that blew only around Katie. It was so strong, it could blow her right out of her body . . . *and into someone else's*!

The first time the magic wind blew, it turned Katie into Speedy, her third-grade class's pet hamster. Katie spent the whole morning going round and round on a hamster wheel and chewing on Speedy's wooden chew sticks. They didn't taste very good at all.

But the chew sticks didn't taste nearly as bad as the food in the school cafeteria used to taste. Katie had seen— and *smelled*—that up close the time the magic wind turned her into Lucille the lunch lady. That time, Katie started a food fight in the cafeteria, but it was Lucille who got fired. Luckily, Katie was able to think of a way to help Lucille get her job back—and to get healthier, tastier food in the cafeteria.

No, Katie *definitely* didn't trust wishes anymore. *Especially* a wish like the one Kevin had just made. After all, who would want a giant king cockroach roaming the halls of Cherrydale Elementary School?

"Okay, all you busy bees," Mr. G. called out, shaking Katie from her thoughts. "Everyone take a seat. I have something really interesting to tell you."

The kids all scrambled into their beanbags. Katie looked up excitedly. She couldn't wait to hear what cool thing Mr. G. had come up with for them to do.

"You all know, it's science week at school. And this year, in addition to your science fair projects, each grade is going to do a special group project. The fourth grade project is— drum roll, please—"

The kids smacked their hands against their legs like drums.

"We're going to clean up the field behind the school," Mr. G. finished.

The kids all stopped drumming and stared at him.

"That doesn't sound like fun," George said.

"I hate cleaning up," Kadeem Carter added. "Just ask my mother."

"What does cleaning the field have to do with science?" Mandy Banks asked.

"It's *environmental* science," Mr. G. explained. "We're helping to protect the squirrels, chipmunks, birds, and mice who live in the field."

Katie would do just about anything to help animals. But even *she* wasn't too happy about having to spend time picking up garbage.

"This really stinks," Andrew groaned.

"It doesn't stink as bad as that garbage is going to," Kevin told him.

"Can't we do something more fun?" George asked their teacher.

Mr. G. smiled. "I'm sure you can find a way to make this fun, George," he said. "You always do."

Katie shook her head. Mr. G. probably shouldn't have said that. Giving George permission to have fun in school could be pretty dangerous.

Chapter 3

"Jessica and I are definitely going to win a blue ribbon for our ladybug project," Suzanne Lock boasted as she and Katie carried their cafeteria trays over to a table at lunchtime.

Katie frowned. Suzanne was her best friend, but sometimes Katie couldn't stand how stuck-up she acted.

"There are a lot of really good science projects out there," Katie reminded her. "Emma W. and I spent all day Saturday in the Cherrydale library researching lightning bugs."

"Jessica and I haven't started our research yet," Suzanne told Katie. "But we did go to the mall to buy matching dresses with black and red polka dots. We're going to wear them at the science fair. We'll look like ladybugs!"

Katie had a feeling that the science fair judges would be more interested in facts than fashion. But she didn't tell Suzanne that. Instead, she turned her attention to her other best friend, Jeremy Fox.

"Did Ms. Sweet tell your class about the fourth-grade project?" she asked him.

"Yeah," Jeremy groaned. "A whole afternoon of picking up candy wrappers, paper cups, and soda cans. Ugh."

"I saw an old, used baby diaper in that field once," Manny Gonzalez said. "It stunk!"

"Gross. Not while I'm eating," George groaned.

Katie rolled her eyes. Nothing anyone had said was more disgusting than what George was doing right then with his food. He had been busy mushing together hot dog pieces, mustard, chocolate pudding, and ketchup.

"Picking up garbage sounds like a really boring project," Suzanne said. "I wish we could do something more interesting."

George looked at her. "We could *make it* more interesting," he suggested.

"How?" Suzanne asked him.

"We could make it a contest," George told her. "The class that picks up the most trash wins."

"Wins what?" Suzanne wondered.

George looked down at the mess of food on his plate. "The losing class has to buy the winning class pizza for lunch," George told her.

"George, that could get expensive," Emma W. reminded him.

"Not for us," George assured her. "Class 4A will win. We win at everything."

"You do not," Jeremy and Suzanne said in unison.

"Class 4B won last week's soccer game," Becky Stern reminded everyone. "Thanks to you, Jeremy," she added with a smile.

Jeremy blushed.

"So is it a bet?" George asked the kids in 4B.

"You're on," Suzanne answered for the class.

George smiled and shook Suzanne's hand.

"Can we stop talking about garbage?" Miriam Chan asked. "It's bad enough we have to look at bugs all day in class. I'm tired of thinking about gross things."

"Just be glad you're not Selena Sanchez," Suzanne told her. "She's using mice in her

science project. I'd rather make a bug out of papier-mâché than work with real live mice."

"Ooh," Miriam groaned. "I hate mice. They have creepy eyes and those long, stringy tails."

"I saw Selena bringing them into the science room today. She had them in a little wire cage." Suzanne shuddered. "They were disgusting."

Katie gasped. "Selena is using live animals in her project?"

"I guess so," Suzanne told her. "Why else would she have brought a cage full of live mice to school? They aren't exactly fashion accessories."

Usually, Katie would have told Suzanne not to be so nasty. But right now she was too upset to worry about anything her best friend did or said. She shot out of her chair and headed toward the other side of the cafeteria.

"Katie, where are you going?" Miriam called after her.

Katie pointed to a table in the far corner

of the cafeteria, where some older kids were sitting and eating their lunches. "I'm going to talk to Selena," she explained.

All of the fourth-graders gasped.

"But Katie, that's the *sixth-grade table!*" Jeremy exclaimed.

"Sixth-graders never talk to fourth-graders," Suzanne added. "They're going to laugh at you if you go over there."

Katie knew that was probably true. The sixth-graders were the oldest kids in the school. They had all their classes on the top floor of the school—where there was no one else but sixth-graders. They always sat together in one corner of the cafeteria. Katie had even once heard them say that all the kids in the school except for them were babies.

But Katie didn't care if the big kids called her a baby. She was going over to that table, and she was going to talk to Selena, no matter what.

She had to. The mice needed her!

Chapter 4

"What do *you* want?" Mickey, one of
the sixth-graders, shouted at Katie as she
approached their table.

Katie gulped. Of course she had seen all
the sixth-graders up close in the schoolyard.
But it was kind of scary walking up to them
all together like this. The sixth-graders were
so big. If they got really mad at her, they
could squash her like a bug—a fourth-grade
bug.

"Selena," Katie said finally in a shaky
voice. "Are you really using mice for your
science fair project?"

A tall, thin girl with big brown eyes and

stick-straight black hair glanced over in Katie's direction. "You're Katie, right?" she asked her.

Katie nodded, surprised. She had no idea that any of the sixth-graders actually knew her name.

"How did you hear about my science project?" Selena asked her.

"My friend Suzanne saw you bringing mice to school in a cage," Katie explained. "We just figured you were using them for your project."

"Ooh, the little kids are getting *so* smart," a short, freckle-faced boy joked. "Did you guys figure that out all by yourselves?"

"Good one, Zack," Mickey chuckled.

Katie frowned. The boys were being really mean.

"I am using mice," Selena told Katie.

"That's not very nice," Katie replied, trying hard to be brave.

"I'm not hurting them," Selena assured Katie. "I'm just giving them a test."

"A test?" Katie asked, confused.

Selena nodded. "Each of the mice has a maze to run through. At the end of one maze is a bottle of sugar water. At the end of the next maze there's a piece of cheese. And at the end of the last maze, there's some mouse food. I want to know if the mice will move faster if they know there's a certain kind of food at the end of the maze. They'll get treats. I'm being nice to them."

"I don't think you're being nice," Katie disagreed. "You're *making* the mice be part of your experiment. You didn't give them a choice. What if they don't like running through mazes?"

Mickey started to laugh. "What's she supposed to do? Ask the mice if they want to be part of her science project?" He turned to Zack. "Hey, little mouse. Do you want to run for the cheese?"

"Squeak, squeak!" Zack answered, trying to sound like a mouse.

The boys started to laugh.

Katie could feel her cheeks burning red.
She hated it when people made fun of her.

"Isn't there a different project you and your
partner could do?" Katie insisted. "Something
without animals?"

"I'm not working with a partner," Selena said, suddenly sounding kind of annoyed.

"Because no one else thinks mice should be used in a science project?" Katie asked.

"No," Selena replied. "Because I wanted to do my project on my own. Look, Katie, my science project isn't any of your business."

"Why don't you go back to your *fourth-*grade table," Mickey added. He folded up his brown paper lunch bag and shot it into a nearby trash can. "Score!" he exclaimed.

"Let's go outside and shoot some real hoops," Zack suggested.

"Sounds good to me," Selena agreed. She stood and walked away with Zack and Mickey. The other sixth-graders at the table soon followed, leaving Katie standing there all alone.

"This isn't over," Katie muttered to herself as she watched them go. "Selena has to learn to be nice to mice!"

Chapter 5

"I've got all of our note cards in my back-pack," Emma W. said as she and Katie walked out of school later that afternoon. "We're going to make a great poster."

"I know," Katie said. "But first I—"

Katie never got to finish her sentence. She stopped talking to focus on what was going on outside the school. Jeremy, Becky, Manny, Miriam, and Jessica were exercising right on the front steps.

Suzanne was there, too. But she wasn't exercising. She was screaming out orders. "One, two! One, two!" she shouted.

"What are you guys doing?" Katie asked her.

"We're getting in shape for the contest tomorrow," Suzanne told her.

"That's a great idea. It's going to be hard work," Katie said, joining in with her friends.

"Katie, you can't practice with us. You're the enemy," Suzanne told her.

"What?"

"She means you're in the other class," Jeremy explained kindly. He frowned. "Suzanne, why are you so mean?"

"Just keep practicing," Suzanne ordered.

Emma W. linked her arm through Katie's.

"Forget about them," she said. "We've got work to do, anyway."

"You're right," Katie agreed. But as she walked away she had a worried look on her face. Once again, it seemed like there was trouble brewing in the fourth grade.

✕ ✕ ✕

"Katie, don't you think we should finish our science fair poster before you do that?" Emma W. suggested as the girls sat in Katie's kitchen later that afternoon.

They were supposed to be working on their lightning bug poster. But Katie had spent her time making other posters instead.

"I'm almost finished," Katie assured her. She picked up a red marker and drew a huge exclamation point on the piece of construction paper she had in front of her. "There. Doesn't that look good?" she asked, holding up the sign.

MICE ARE PEOPLE TOO!

"Selena's going to be mad if you put that up

at school," Emma said.

Katie already knew that. But it didn't matter. She was doing this to help the mice. "I'm going to put these posters up all over school. When people find out what Selena is doing, I think they'll get angry and ask her to stop. If other people talk to her about—"

"I really don't think Selena's doing anything that bad," Emma interrupted. "Didn't she say that the mice were going to get treats if they ran through the mazes?"

"Who says they *want* treats?" Katie replied.

"Come on, Katie," Emma said. "Animals love treats!"

Just then, Katie's cocker spaniel, Pepper, began to bark.

Katie walked over to the kitchen cabinet and pulled out a green doggie cookie. "Sit," she told Pepper. "Give me your paw."

Pepper sat back on his hind legs. He lifted one of his brown-and-white paws.

Katie shook his paw. "Good boy," she said as she handed him his treat.

"How come you make Pepper sit before he gets a treat?" Emma asked Katie.

"He's supposed to work for it," Katie explained.

"Kind of like what Selena's mice will have to do at the science fair, huh?" Emma pointed out.

"I'm not making Pepper be part of a science project," Katie argued.

Emma took a deep breath. "*We're* not going to *have* a project for the science fair if you don't stop worrying about mice, and start thinking about lightning bugs. The science fair is just two days away!"

"Okay," Katie agreed. "Let's go print out some lightning bug pictures from the computer. But I'm not giving up on helping those poor little mice. Not yet."

Chapter 6

The next morning, Katie brought an armful of posters to school with her. But not the lightning bug poster. Emma was bringing that. Katie was carrying her own posters.

Katie had left her house really early, so the schoolyard was empty when she arrived. "Perfect," she said as she pulled a poster out of her bag and taped it to a tree.

By the time the other kids got to school, there were posters taped to many of the trees.

BE NICE TO MICE!

MICE ARE PEOPLE TOO!

MICE DON'T BELONG IN SCIENCE PROJECTS!

"Hey, who put those up?" Katie heard Mickey ask as he and Zack arrived at school and saw the posters.

"Man, Selena's gonna be mad!" Zack exclaimed.

"Yeah," Mickey agreed. "And when Selena gets mad, things can get ugly."

Katie gulped. That did not sound good at all.

Just then, Selena arrived. She took one look at Katie's posters and frowned angrily. She reached up, and yanked one of them down from the tree. Then she crumpled it up into a tight ball, and threw it in the trash.

"Hey—" Katie began. Then she stopped herself, remembering what Mickey and Zack had said. Maybe it was better that Selena didn't know who put up the posters.

Besides, by now, everyone had already seen them. That was all that mattered.

× × ×

"What are you guys carrying in those backpacks?" Mandy Banks asked George and Kevin a few minutes later, as the kids walked into class 4A.

"Nothing," George told her.

"They sure look full," Mandy said suspiciously.

Katie looked at the boys. Mandy was right. Their backpacks were bulging.

"It's for our science project," George explained. "No big deal."

Katie didn't believe *that* for a minute. She could tell by the way Kevin and George were

guarding their backpacks that whatever was in there was definitely a big deal to them.

"This morning we will all go set up our projects in the gym," Mr. G. told the class. "And then after lunch, it's off to the big field cleanup. Are you ready?"

"Not as ready as 4B," Andrew said. "They practiced for it all yesterday afternoon."

"We're going to lose," Mandy moaned.

"There aren't any losers in this," Mr. G. told her. He looked seriously at the class. "Ms. Sweet and I have heard about your contest. We both want our classes to remember that this is about cleaning up the environment, not winning a pizza."

"We're gonna win anyway," George assured him.

"How can you be so sure?" Emma Stavros asked.

"Trust me," George told her.

Katie sighed. Trusting George wasn't always the easiest thing to do.

Chapter 7

"This is the perfect spot for our lightning bug," Emma W. said later that morning as she and Katie set up their science fair table in the gym. "It's just dark enough here for our flashlight to glow really brightly."

Katie nodded. "Now let's find a good spot on the wall for this," she said as she lifted up their lightning bug fact poster and taped it up.

Katie stepped back to admire the poster the girls had created together. She and Emma had sprinkled shimmery glitter on a drawing of a lightning bug. The glitter made it look as though the lightning bug's tail was all lit up. The drawing was surrounded by photographs of real lightning bugs eating, flying, and lighting up a dark sky. The pictures were labeled with interesting facts, like:

Lightning bugs use their lights to warn their enemies that they taste too bad to be eaten.

Adult lightning bugs eat other insects and sometimes nectar.

Lightning bugs are happiest living in warm, humid places, like those near lakes and streams.

"I think our poster looks really nice," Emma said.

"I hope the judges think so, too," Katie replied. She looked around the gym. It sure was noisy. The whole school was in there at the same time. All the kids were having fun, but Katie could also tell they were all working hard. Everyone wanted to get a blue ribbon at the fair.

Katie knew winning a prize could be tough. There were lots of good projects, like the solar system a pair of second-graders had made from fruits and vegetables, the volcano that really exploded that two third-graders had built, and the guess-the-smell game a pair of fifth-graders had created as part of their five senses project.

But Katie thought that the sixth-grade projects were the most interesting. Sixth-graders were allowed to research anything they wanted.

Bryce had placed one of her baby teeth in a cup of cola to show how the cola rots your teeth. Justine and Risa had created a miniature rain forest in a jar, with real plants and water. Mickey and Zack had built a robot that could really walk and talk.

As Katie was looking around, she noticed that one project wasn't there—Selena's!

Wow! Katie thought excitedly. *Maybe Selena has changed her mind about her project. Maybe she's in the library right now, coming up with something else to display tomorrow.*

Suddenly, Katie felt very powerful . . . for a fourth-grader, anyway.

Chapter 8

"Okay, you guys, let's all line up," Mr. G. said as class 4A walked out onto the field behind the schoolyard later that day. "We'll form a human chain, walking from each end of the field to the middle, picking up every piece of trash we find."

Class 4A lined up on one side of the field. Class 4B lined up on the other side. The plan was for the kids in each class to pick up trash and put it in huge garbage bags. When they met in the middle, the field would be clean!

"George, Kevin? Don't you think it would be a lot easier to pick up the trash if you put down those heavy backpacks first?" Mr. G. asked.

Katie looked toward the end of the line. She

was surprised to see that George and Kevin had brought their backpacks outside.

"We're cool," George assured their teacher.

"Yeah," Kevin agreed. "We need these. They're filled with . . . ow," Kevin stopped and stared at George. "What'd you kick me for?"

"They're filled with important stuff we don't want to let go of," George finished Kevin's sentence.

"Okay, suit yourselves," Mr. G. said. He smiled at the kids in class 4A. "Now, is everyone wearing their gloves?"

The kids held up their hands.

"Cool," Mr. G. said. "Dudes, get cleaning!"

"This is disgusting," Emma S. muttered as she placed a used paper cup in a trash bag.

"Yuck," Andrew groaned as he picked up a smelly milk container.

"The animals are lucky we're here to clean up their habitat," Katie said cheerfully.

"How come you're so happy?" Kadeem asked her.

"I'm just in a good mood," Katie replied.

Even though they were picking up trash, she
was glad to be outside. After all, they were
helping the animals in the field. More
importantly, she was pretty sure she had saved
three little mice from being part of a science
project.

This was a really good day. The only thing
that could make it better would be if class 4A
could win the pizza contest, too.

But that would mean a lot of hard work from
everyone in the class. And right now, George

and Kevin sure didn't seem to be doing their part. They were sitting in the grass, whispering to each other and laughing. That made Katie really angry.

"Those guys are such jerks," Mandy said as she bent down to pick up a soda bottle.

"George is the one who made the bet in the first place. He's not even helping us," Kadeem pointed out.

Katie frowned. George and Kevin were definitely not being fair. She stomped over to where they were sitting to tell them so.

"How come you guys aren't helping?" she demanded.

"We're finished," George told her.

"We collected lots of garbage." Kevin pointed to a nearby garbage bag. It was completely full.

"See, Katie Kazoo?" George said, using the nickname he'd given her back in third grade. "We've got this contest in the bag."

Chapter 9

About an hour later, the field was clean. It was time to see which class had picked up the most trash.

"I think it's easy to see who is going to be eating pizza at lunch after the science fair tomorrow," Kevin boasted.

Class 4A had filled four bags of garbage. Class 4B had only filled two.

"We want pepperoni on our pizzas," George told Suzanne. Then he glanced over at Katie. "No, make that half pepperoni and half vegetables."

Katie smiled gratefully.

Suzanne *wasn't* smiling. She hated losing.

"You cheated," she insisted.

"How?" Mandy asked. "We picked up more garbage than you did! What do you think is in those bags? Grass?"

"Suzanne's right," Jeremy agreed. "The field wasn't *that* dirty. There's no way you could have collected that much junk."

"I agree with Jeremy," Becky said.

"You *always* agree with Jeremy," George argued. "You have a crush on him."

"Shut up, George," Jeremy said.

Katie frowned. She couldn't believe what sore losers the kids in Class 4B were being.

"You guys owe us pizza," George demanded. "And you're going to get it for us."

"George, calm down," Mr. G. said. "It's just pizza."

"This isn't fair!" Suzanne declared again. She kicked at one of the giant garbage bags. It burst open, and some of the garbage began falling out.

"Suzanne," Ms. Sweet scolded. She handed

her another garbage bag. "Please pick up that trash."

Suzanne frowned, but she took the bag. She knew better than to argue with a teacher—even one as nice as Ms. Sweet.

Everyone stood around watching Suzanne pick up the trash all by herself. A few of the boys began to snicker.

"I'll help you," Katie said, feeling sorry for her friend. She bent down and began picking up some of the spilled trash.

"Me too," Jessica said. She picked up a torn piece of a magazine cover and began to put it in the bag. She stopped as something on the cover caught her eye.

"Kevin, this is addressed to *your* house," Jessica remarked. "You're a litter bug!"

Kevin bit his lip and kicked at the ground.

Suzanne glanced at the piece of notebook paper in her hand. "George, this has *your* name on it. It's your spelling test!" She looked down and laughed. "Sixty-three. That's pretty bad, George."

George glared at her.

Suzanne began looking more closely at the garbage. "Hey, *all* of this stuff has Kevin and George's names and addresses on it," she said.

Katie stared at the boys in amazement. So that was what they had been hiding in their backpacks!

"This isn't garbage from the field," Suzanne told George and Kevin. "It's from your houses." Suzanne ran over and started opening up garbage bags.

"What are you doing?" Kevin asked her.

"Proving that you cheated!" Suzanne said.

Jessica went over to help Suzanne. "Look, these are from last month's science unit," she said, holding up a pile of notebook paper and showing them to Kevin. "And they have your sloppy handwriting on them."

"That's it!" Suzanne exclaimed. "You cheated, so you're disqualified. Class 4B wins!"

Katie turned and scowled at Kevin and George. Class 4A had lost the bet, and it was all their fault. The other kids in the class were really angry, too.

"I can't believe you guys," Andrew moaned.

"You are so lazy," Emma S. added.

Usually, Katie would have been upset that everyone was picking on George and Kevin. But today she wasn't upset at all. George and Kevin hadn't cared a bit about cleaning up the field so the animals could have a clean place to live. So why should Katie care if they got yelled at?

Finally, Mr. G. stepped in. "Okay, everyone, that's enough. Ms. Sweet and I think you're all winners. You worked very hard."

"Except for George and Kevin," Jeremy reminded him.

Mr. G. nodded. "That's true. And don't worry. I think I know a way that they can do some cleaning up, too," he said mysteriously.

George and Kevin gulped.

"But the rest of you deserve a reward," Mr. G. continued. "So you can all have pizza for lunch tomorrow." He turned to George and Kevin. "Except for you two," he added. "You'll have the school lunch. Tuna surprise."

"Oh, man," Kevin moaned. "I hate tuna surprise."

George frowned. "Me too. It tastes like garbage."

Suzanne looked at the pile of envelopes, papers, and magazine covers on the ground. "That's just perfect," she said with a laugh.

Chapter 10

WELCOME TO THE SCIENCE FAIR!

Katie felt all tingly as she spotted the big banner in the gym the next morning. She was so excited. The big day had arrived. In just about half an hour, the parents would be arriving, and the science teachers would start the judging.

"I can't wait until my parents get here," Katie told Emma W.

"My dad can't come. He has a huge meeting this morning. But my mother is coming," Emma said. "And she promised *not* to bring the twins!"

"That's a good thing," Katie agreed. Emma

W. had lots of brothers and sisters. She had a teenaged sister named Lacey, a brother in first grade named Matthew, and one-year-old twin brothers, Tyler and Timmy. The twins were always getting into some sort of trouble.

And trouble was the last thing Katie wanted today. She just wanted to sit back and enjoy the science fair . . . *a science fair without Selena and her mice!*

Unfortunately, Katie didn't always get what she wanted. At that very moment, Selena walked into the room, holding her mice in their cage.

Katie watched as Selena began to set up her mazes. She placed a bottle of sugar water at the end of one. There was a plate filled with brown mouse food at the end of another. At the finish line of the third maze was a hunk of cheese.

Katie was angry. Selena was going ahead with her experiment. She obviously didn't care about those mice!

Unlike Katie, however, Emma was focused on the lightning bug project. "I can't get this flashlight to work," Emma said, shaking the light up and down. "Do you think the batteries are dead?"

Katie shook her head. "They're brand-new," she said, looking away from Selena for a moment.

"This is terrible!" Emma moaned.

Katie thought for a second. "Wait. I have another flashlight. It's on one of the key chains on my book bag. I'll run back to the classroom and get it."

"Great!" Emma exclaimed. "But hurry."

Katie nodded and raced out of the gym. She headed straight down the hall and into 4A.

The room was completely silent. Nobody was there—except Slinky, the class snake, of course. He wasn't allowed at the science fair. It was for people only.

People, and Selena's mice, Katie thought angrily.

But there was no time to worry about that now. Katie had to get her flashlight. She walked over to her book bag and began to pry the key chain loose.

Suddenly, Katie felt a cool breeze blowing on the back of her neck. She looked around the room. All the windows were shut. None of the paper bugs flying from the ceiling were moving around.

The wind seemed to be blowing just on Katie. The magic wind was back!

"Oh, no!" Katie exclaimed. "Not right before the science fair!"

But the magic wind didn't care if Katie missed the science fair. It picked up speed, blowing harder and harder. WHOOSH! Katie was sure it would blow her away. She shut her eyes tight, and tried not to cry.

And then it stopped. Just like that. The magic wind was gone. And so was Katie Carew.

She'd turned into somebody else.

But who?

Chapter 11

Squeak, squeak, squeak.

That was the first thing Katie heard as the magic wind faded away. Slowly, she opened her eyes. There, on the table in front of her was a big wire cage with three white mice inside.

Katie gulped. She was standing in the middle of the science fair, right in front of Selena's display table.

That could mean only one thing.

The magic wind had turned Katie into Selena!

Katie frowned. This was so not fair! She didn't want to be Selena. She wanted to be Katie Carew. She wanted to be able to stand in front of her lightning bug poster, and proudly tell her parents and the other visitors all about what lightning bugs eat and where they live.

She did not want to be making these poor mice run through mazes.

But Katie *was* Selena now. And as much as she hated the idea, she was going to have to do Selena's project.

Slowly, Katie lifted off the top of the cage and reached her hand in. The mice scurried away from her grasp.

I was right, Katie thought. *They* don't *want to do this*. Suddenly she didn't care if Selena had a project at the fair or not. All she cared about was the mice. And *they* sure looked miserable all huddled up in a corner of the cage.

Katie took her hand out of the cage stood back. Almost immediately, the mice began running around and around. In less than a second they had scurried up the wire side of the cage and out the top.

Katie watched as the three mice ran free around the table. Katie smiled. "I knew you didn't want to run in those mazes," she told them. "You just wanted to play."

Suddenly, all three mice scurried down one of the table legs and onto the floor.

"Wait," Katie called after them. "You were just supposed to hang out on the table for a while!"

But mice don't just hang out. They run . . . fast. Katie grabbed the cage and took off. "Wait!" she cried out again as she raced to catch the speeding mice.

But the mice were faster than Katie was. They sped off in different directions around the gym.

"EEEEEEEK!!!!!! A mouse!" A third-grader shouted out.

"Aaaah! There's a mouse on my project!" Miriam Chan screeched.

Everyone seemed to be screaming at once.

Mrs. Hauser, a sixth-grade teacher,

jumped up on a chair. "Selena, catch those mice!" she demanded.

"I'll help you, Selena!" Mickey called to Katie. "I see one over there!" He slid across the floor.

"Ouch!" Justine shouted as Mickey hit her in the leg. "Watch where you're going."

"Sorry," Mickey apologized. "You were in my way."

"Selena, there's a mouse under the fossil table!" Zack screamed.

Katie jumped over to where two scared third-graders were standing at a table behind their fossil projects. She looked down. Sure enough, there was a mouse sitting beneath the table.

"Get that thing away from me!" one of the third-graders shouted.

"Shhh . . ." Katie warned. She crouched down and reached for the mouse. "You'll scare the—"

Crash! As she bent down to catch the

mouse, Katie hit one of the plaster fossils with her rear end. The fossil fell and broke into three pieces. The mouse ran off in fear.

Chapter 12

It seemed like everyone was screaming at the same time. Katie didn't know who to listen to.

"Selena Sanchez, you need to get those mice under control!" Mrs. Hauser shouted from high atop her chair.

"I think I saw one head under the radiator," Mr. Kane, the school principal, called out. He raced across the gym, leaping over the cracked fossil on the floor, and . . . *clang*! He banged his head against a metal volleyball pole. "Ow," he moaned, raising his hand to his forehead.

"There goes a mouse!" Justine shouted.

She leaped up from behind her rain forest project and tried to grab a mouse. "Whoops!" she exclaimed, as she bumped into Bryce's cola and tooth experiment. *Splat.* The warm, brown soda spilled all over the gym floor.

"You ruined my project!" Bryce shouted angrily as she bent to recover the tooth. "Justine, you'll do anything to win a blue ribbon!"

"I was just trying to catch the mouse," Justine insisted. "Whoa, there he goes again!"

"I got him!" Risa shouted, as she scooped the mouse up. "Oh, yuck. He's all sticky from the soda. Here, Selena," she said as she handed Katie the soaked mouse.

"Thanks," Katie said, placing him safely back in the cage and closing the lid.

"Now all I have to do is find the other two."

But that wasn't going to be easy. The gym was so big. And the mice were so small. How would Katie ever find them?

"Aaaaaaahhhhhhhh! A mouse!" a second-grade boy cried out.

That was how! She would just follow the screams.

"There he is, Selena!" Bryce shouted, leaping over one of the tables. And racing toward the second-grade solar system projects. "I'll grab him."

"Careful, Bryce!" Katie shouted out. "You're going to knock over that . . ."

Too late! *Bam!* Bryce bumped into the solar system made of fruit. The planets tumbled to the floor.

Katie spotted the mouse hiding under the table. She took a step toward him and . . . *squish*. She stepped on a tomato.

"You just crushed Mars!" the second-grader screamed. He began to sob. "Waaah!"

"Don't cry," Katie told him. "You can get another tomato from the cafeteria."

The second-grader cried harder. His teacher bent down and tried to help scoop up the squashed tomato. The mouse ran off.

"Selena, over there!" Zack cried. "Near the model volcano!" He ran over and reached across the volcano table to catch the mouse.

KABOOM!

Suddenly, there was a loud explosion as the third-grade volcano project erupted, spitting lava high up in the air.

"Boys! What have you done?" Mrs. Derkman shouted.

Katie looked over at her old third-grade teacher. Mrs. Derkman had been standing right next to the volcano when it had erupted. She was covered in ooey, gooey fake lava!

"This is not funny," Mrs. Derkman scolded the boys.

"It wasn't us," one of the third-graders said. He pointed to Zack. "That sixth-grader hit the remote control button."

"Sorry," Zack apologized to Mrs. Derkman. "I was trying to catch a mouse. It wasn't my fault."

Katie looked around at the soda puddle on the gym floor, the squished tomato, the broken fossil, and the flowing volcano lava.

Zack was right. It wasn't his fault. It was her fault. *All* of it.

Just then Mr. Kane walked over to Katie. "Here you go, Selena," he said, handing Katie one of the mice. "I caught him under the radiator."

"Thank you," Katie said sincerely. She looked at the big, egg-shaped bump above the principal's eye. "Sorry about your head."

"I'll be okay," he assured her. "Just put this mouse in its cage before anything else happens."

"Well, at least you got two of them back," Mickey said to Katie as she placed the mouse in its cage and closed the lid.

"I wonder where the third mouse is?" Zack asked.

Just then, George came running over. He was huffing and puffing really hard. "Selena, I just saw your mouse go out into the hallway. I tried to catch him, but he was too fast. Boy, I hope he wasn't going into class 4A."

"Why?" Mickey asked him.

"We have a snake in our classroom."

"So?" Mickey asked.

"Snakes *eat* mice!" George sounded very proud to know something a sixth-grader didn't.

Katie gulped. What if the mouse really was heading for her classroom? She had to save him!

Quickly, she raced out of the gym.

Chapter 13

"If I were a mouse, where would I hide?" Katie wondered as she walked through the empty hallway.

Before Katie could figure that out, she felt a cool breeze blowing against the back of her neck. Seconds later, the breeze turned into a full-fledged tornado that was spinning only around Katie.

The magic wind blew harder and harder. It whistled wildly in her ears, and blew Serena's long brown hair in her eyes.

And then it stopped. Just like that.

Katie Carew was back.

And so was Selena. She was standing in

the hallway next to Katie. "How did I get out here?" she asked. She sounded very confused.

"You were looking for your mouse," Katie told her.

"Oh, yeah, I remember. Or at least I think I do. It's all kind of fuzzy," Selena said quietly.

"Two of the mice are back in their cage," Katie told her. "We just have to find this one."

"I kind of remember letting the mice out of their cage," Selena muttered. "But that doesn't make sense."

"Why not?" Katie asked her.

"Because I would never do that," Selena explained. "I always take good care of my pets."

Katie's eyes shot open wide. "Your *pets*?"

Selena nodded. "My mice. Larry, Moe, and Curly. I've had them for six months now. And I always keep them safe. At least I did until today."

Suddenly, Katie felt extra-bad. The mice were Selena's *pets*. She obviously loved them

a lot. And now Katie had lost one of them. Maybe even for good!

"My poor little mouse," Selena said. Her eyes welled up with tears. "He's probably scared, and hungry, and thirsty."

Hungry. "That's it!" Katie exclaimed. There was only one place in the school where the mouse would find plenty of food and water. "I'll bet I know where your mouse is, Selena. Follow me!"

× × ×

The cafeteria was empty when Katie and Selena arrived. As Selena checked under the tables and chairs, Katie went back to where Lucille, the lunch lady, had set up the food for today's lunch. The hot food was being kept in the warming trays. The sandwich meats and cheeses were in the refrigerated section.

Katie looked over to where the triangular slices of yellow and white cheese were laid out under plastic wrap. Sure enough, there was a little white mouse standing over the cheese.

Katie stayed very still. She didn't want to scare him away. After all, she might never find him again. Slowly, she reached toward him.

The mouse's little ears shot up at attention. He turned and scampered away. But Katie was fast and determined. She reached out with both hands and . . .

Bam!

The tray crashed to the ground. There were pieces of Muenster, American, and Swiss cheese all over the floor.

Katie didn't care. She'd apologize to Lucille later. She may have dropped the cheese, but she'd caught the mouse!

"Selena!" she called out. "I've got him!"

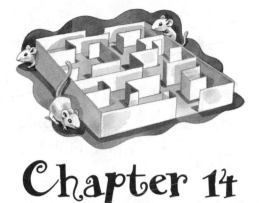

Chapter 14

"Katie, where have you been?" Emma W. asked as Katie walked into the gym. "I've been looking all over for you. The flashlight works after all! We just had the batteries in the wrong way."

Phew! Katie was relieved. After all the excitement, she had totally forgotten about the flashlight.

Katie looked over at Selena's table. A crowd of kids had formed around her. Katie hoped Selena was okay. She decided to go over and find out.

✕   ✕   ✕

"Your mice sure caused a mess," Justine

told Selena as Katie walked over to the table.

"It wasn't their fault. They were just acting like mice," Selena defended them.

"That's right," Katie said, stepping up beside Selena. "If everyone hadn't been screaming and jumping all around, everything would be fine. You people scared them away." Suddenly Katie wasn't so afraid of the sixth-graders. She felt very brave. Especially now that she and Selena were on the same side.

"Don't blame us," Justine argued. "Selena is the one who let them out of their cage."

Katie bit her lip. She knew that wasn't true.

Just then, Mr. G. walked over. Mrs. Hauser came up behind him with a fresh soda for Bryce's tooth experiment.

"Katie, you'd better get back to your lightning bug," Mr. G. said. "The parents will be here any minute." He frowned slightly at Selena's sad expression. "Don't worry," he told her. "Everything's okay now."

Mrs. Hauser nodded in agreement. "The

fossil is glued back together. The tooth is in a fresh cup of cola. Lucille is going to the cafeteria to get a new tomato for the solar system, and the third-graders have put fresh lava into their volcano," she said. "But you need to go set up your mazes."

"I can't ask my mice to run through mazes now," Selena told her teacher. "They're too tired. They've been through too much!"

"If you don't do your experiment, I can't give you a grade," Mrs. Hauser reminded her. "You don't want a zero, do you?"

Selena bit her lip. "No. But I can't make my mice do this, either."

Mrs. Hauser thought for a minute. "I understand," she said finally. "How about you do a research paper instead? Maybe something about animals?"

"Okay," Selena replied. "I'll start on it this weekend."

Wow! Katie was very impressed. Selena loved her mice so much, she was willing to do extra work rather than make them do some more running. Selena really cared about animals and their rights after all.

Katie had been very wrong about Selena. She wished there was some way she could help her.

Chapter 15

"I can't believe Jessica and I didn't get a ribbon today," Suzanne moaned later that afternoon, as she and Katie walked together in the Cherrydale Mall. "We looked so awesome in our ladybug dresses."

Katie knew that wasn't the point of a science fair. But she couldn't explain that to Suzanne. Especially since Katie and Emma W. had won the third-place ribbon for the fourth grade. Suzanne would just think Katie was bragging.

"You want to get a snack?" she asked Suzanne, changing the subject.

Suzanne shook her head. "I'm still full

from the pizza we ate for lunch. Did you see the look on George's face when I slid my slice right under his nose?"

"That was kind of mean," Katie told her.

"Not as mean as his cheating," Suzanne answered her.

Katie turned her head. Something exciting caught her eye. Rows and rows of wire animal crates had been set up in the middle of the mall. Inside each crate was a kitten or a cat. Nearby, volunteers were walking dogs. The dogs all wore coats that read, "Please Adopt Me."

"The Cherrydale Animal Shelter is having one of their pet adoption days!" Katie exclaimed.

"You're really crazy about that animal shelter," Suzanne remarked.

"Of course I am. That's where I found Pepper," Katie reminded Suzanne. "I got him when he . . ."

". . . was just a puppy," Suzanne finished

Katie's sentence for her. "I know. *Everybody* knows. You tell that story all the time."

Katie couldn't argue with that. She did talk about Pepper an awful lot. Suzanne didn't have any pets. She couldn't understand how special they could be.

But Selena understood. Katie learned that today.

Just thinking about Selena made Katie sad. She was probably sitting in the library working on her research paper. And here Katie was, having fun in the mall.

Just then, one of the volunteer dog walkers strolled near to where Katie and Suzanne were standing. Katie looked at the volunteer with surprise.

"Selena!" she exclaimed. "What are you doing here? I thought you would be in the library."

Selena looked at her curiously. "Hi, Katie," she said. "Why would you think that?"

"Well, you have that research paper to do

and I just thought . . ." Katie began.

Selena frowned. "I know. I have to start on
that. But I volunteered to help with the pet
adoptions this afternoon. I couldn't let the
animals down."

"Do you work at the shelter?" Suzanne
asked.

Selena nodded. "Just once a week."

"I didn't know kids could work there," Katie said.

"You have to be twelve years old to volunteer," Selena explained. "I just turned twelve last month."

"What kind of things do they let you do?" Katie asked.

"I walk the dogs. I play with them a lot, too," Selena replied.

"That sounds like a great job!" Katie said. "I'd like to do that when I'm twelve."

"Maybe you won't have to wait," Selena told Katie. She pointed over to where some of the puppies were. "Those two boys are your age, and they're helping out."

Katie turned and looked toward where Suzanne was pointing. "George! Kevin!" she exclaimed. "What are you doing here?"

George looked at Katie. He held out a long wooden stick with a scoop on the end. "What does it look like we're doing?" he asked her. "We're scooping up any poop the dogs make on the floor."

"Wow! I didn't know you guys were so into helping out animals," Katie said.

"We're not," Kevin assured her. "This is Mr. G.'s idea. It's to make up for not helping to clean up the field." He frowned as a puppy who was too young to have been trained squatted down to go to the bathroom. "Man, I hate these dogs," he moaned.

"*I* love them," Selena told him. "They're very special. It would be nice to find places for all of them."

Katie thought about that for a minute. "Maybe you can," she suggested. "And do your research paper at the same time."

Selena looked at her curiously.

"Suzanne and

I have this website called *Reading Rocks*," Katie explained. "We work on it with our friend Emma. Every month we review a new book. Lots of people have been checking it out."

"What does that have to do with getting shelter animals adopted or my research paper?" Selena asked the girls.

"Nothing," Suzanne said. "I have no idea what Katie is thinking. I never do."

Selena laughed.

Katie scowled. "Let me finish, Suzanne." she said. "We could post pictures of the dogs. You can do research about each dog like, like what breed it is, or if it's a mutt, you could write about all the different breeds they are. Then you could suggest the type of family that would be best for each dog."

"I'll bet Mrs. Hauser would love for me to do that for my research project," Selena said with a grin. "I've got to get that done by the end of next week. How about I research ten dogs? Then you can post their pictures on your website!"

"Great!" Katie agreed.

"We should start with Cody, here." Selena patted the big brown-and-white dog she had been walking. "Let's get him a home first."

"All right!" Katie exclaimed. Lots of animals were going to find homes now—all because of her idea.

When it came to great ideas, Katie was definitely the champ. Not even the magic wind could change that.

Bug Facts

Do you want to be a bug expert like the kids in 4A? Katie and her friends are giving you the buzz on what's cool about bugs.

- There are more insects on Earth than any other type of animal. Ninety-five percent of all animal species on Earth are insects.
- Houseflies find sugar with their feet, which are ten million times more sensitive than human tongues.
- Ants can lift and carry objects that are fifty times their own weight.
- Mosquitoes are twice as attracted to the color blue than any other color.

- The world's fastest insect is the dragon-fly. It can fly at a speed of thirty-six miles per hour, which is faster than cars are allowed to go on some city streets.